Disney

BEAUTY AND THE BEAST

the ENCHANTMENT

By ERIC GERON

Screenplay by EVAN SPILIOTOPOULOS
and STEPHEN CHBOSKY and BILL CONDON

 PRESS

LOS ANGELES • NEW YORK

Printed in the United States of America

First Paperback Edition, January 2017

3 5 7 9 10 8 6 4 2

Library of Congress Control Number: 2016952968

ISBN 978-1-4847-8283-5

FAC-029261-17020

For more Disney Press fun, visit www.disneybooks.com

For more *Beauty and the Beast* fun, visit www.disney.com/beautyandthebeast

*I*n the heart of France, there lived a prince with no love in his heart. The Prince was handsome. But despite having everything he could ever have wanted, he was selfish and terribly unkind.

One dark and stormy night, the Prince threw a party and invited only guests he deemed as handsome as himself.

Suddenly, an old beggar woman entered the castle. She offered a red rose to the Prince in exchange for shelter from the storm. The Prince turned her away.

The old beggar woman revealed that she was actually an enchantress. She knew that the Prince could not see past appearances. As punishment, she turned him into a horrible beast and his subjects into household objects. The enchantment also made the villagers completely forget the castle and all who lived there.

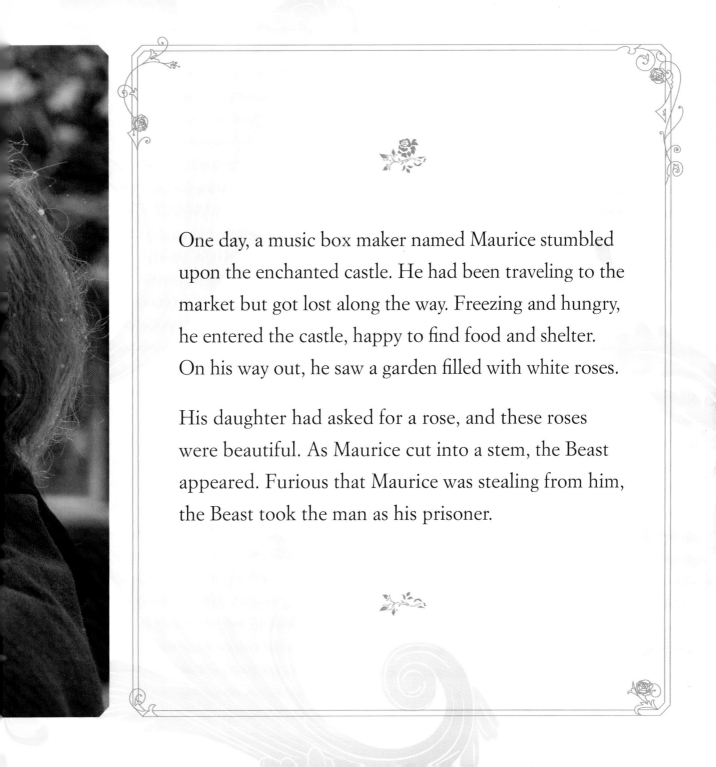

One day, a music box maker named Maurice stumbled upon the enchanted castle. He had been traveling to the market but got lost along the way. Freezing and hungry, he entered the castle, happy to find food and shelter. On his way out, he saw a garden filled with white roses.

His daughter had asked for a rose, and these roses were beautiful. As Maurice cut into a stem, the Beast appeared. Furious that Maurice was stealing from him, the Beast took the man as his prisoner.

Maurice's daughter, Belle, was a smart, kind, and brave young woman, as beautiful on the inside as she was on the outside. She had always dreamed of something more than her small town could offer. When her father failed to return from his trip, Belle set out to find him.

At the enchanted castle, Belle discovered her father locked up in a dark prison tower. Then she met the Beast and decided she would rescue her father herself. Against her father's wishes, she took his place as prisoner. She assured him she was not afraid. She would find a way out.

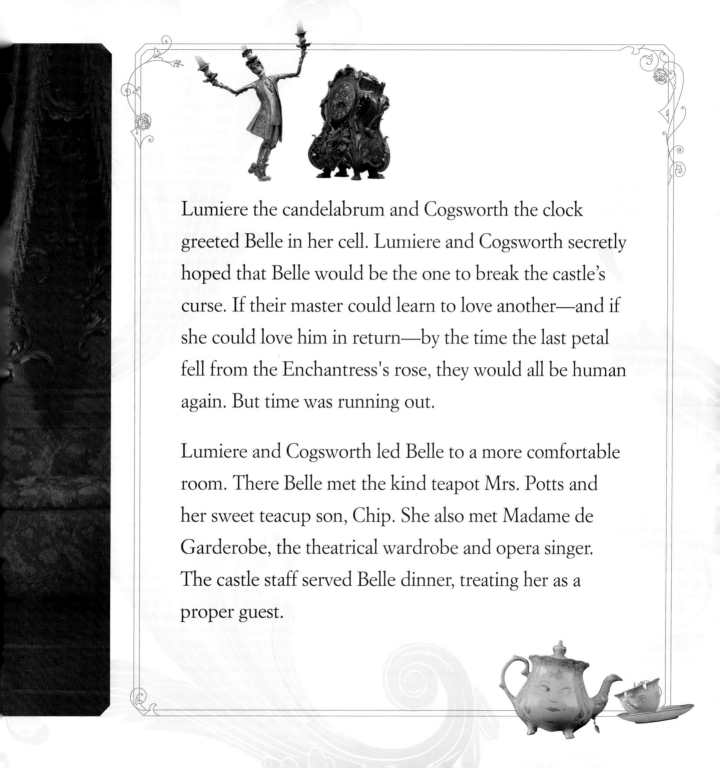

Lumiere the candelabrum and Cogsworth the clock greeted Belle in her cell. Lumiere and Cogsworth secretly hoped that Belle would be the one to break the castle's curse. If their master could learn to love another—and if she could love him in return—by the time the last petal fell from the Enchantress's rose, they would all be human again. But time was running out.

Lumiere and Cogsworth led Belle to a more comfortable room. There Belle met the kind teapot Mrs. Potts and her sweet teacup son, Chip. She also met Madame de Garderobe, the theatrical wardrobe and opera singer. The castle staff served Belle dinner, treating her as a proper guest.

After dinner, Belle snuck off to the West Wing of the castle, where she discovered the Enchantress's rose and a portrait of the Prince painted before his curse. The Beast stormed in, enraged that she had trespassed in his private quarters. Belle had had enough. She fled the castle. During her escape, wolves attacked her, but the Beast arrived in the nick of time to fight them off. He was injured in the struggle, so Belle helped him get back to the castle.

She cleaned a large gash on the Beast's arm. His subjects were eternally grateful that Belle had helped him. Lumiere and Cogsworth explained the enchantment to Belle—but kept her potential role in it a secret.

Meanwhile, Belle was being enchanted in other ways. Once the Beast realized that he and Belle shared a love of reading, he showed her his favorite place in the castle. It was the biggest private library in all of France, lined with books from floor to ceiling. Belle was delighted.

That night, the two, each reading a book, shared a quiet dinner at the table. Looking up from the pages, Belle watched the Beast plant his face in his bowl and slurp up his soup. The Beast's table manners made Belle smile.

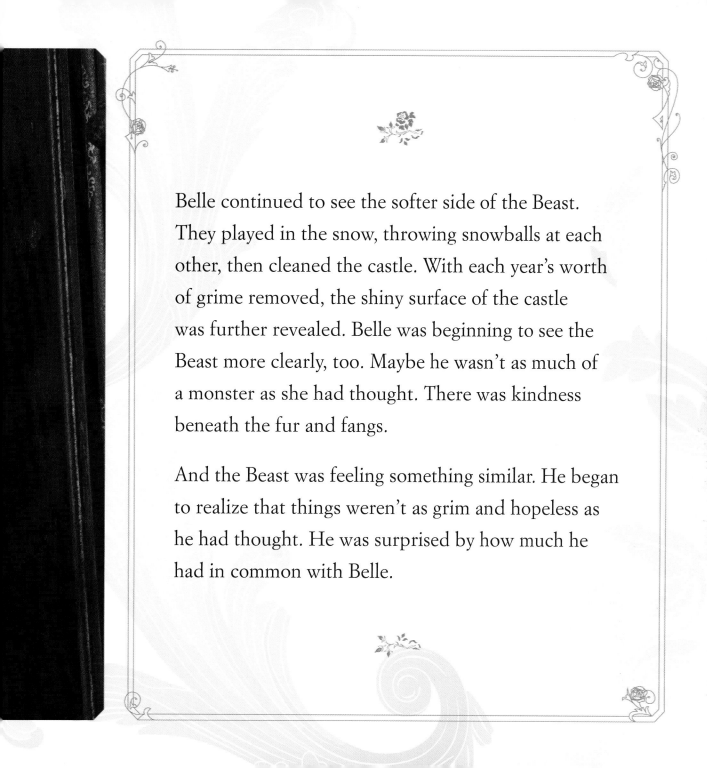

Belle continued to see the softer side of the Beast. They played in the snow, throwing snowballs at each other, then cleaned the castle. With each year's worth of grime removed, the shiny surface of the castle was further revealed. Belle was beginning to see the Beast more clearly, too. Maybe he wasn't as much of a monster as she had thought. There was kindness beneath the fur and fangs.

And the Beast was feeling something similar. He began to realize that things weren't as grim and hopeless as he had thought. He was surprised by how much he had in common with Belle.

One night, the Beast revealed to his staff that he had strong feelings for Belle. But he felt she deserved to fall in love with someone better than him. He met Belle in the ballroom, which had been restored to its former glory. He and Belle danced gracefully and shared a special evening together.

Belle admitted that she missed her father. The Beast gave her his magic mirror. In it, she could see her father being bullied by the villagers. The Beast encouraged Belle to go help him. He loved her and knew he had to set her free. The Beast only wished he could have done the same for his enchanted subjects.

In the village, Belle fearlessly faced those who tormented her father. Maurice had told them that Belle was trapped in the enchanted castle with the Beast, but they thought he was out of his mind. To prove her father had spoken the truth, Belle revealed the Beast to the villagers through the magic mirror.

Belle's plan backfired: the villagers set off and stormed the enchanted castle. The Beast's subjects defended themselves, sending the villagers running. The villain Gaston tried to kill the Beast but met his own end. Belle raced to the Beast's side. He had been badly injured. Meanwhile, all the Beast's subjects began to lose their remaining human traits as the last petal of the Enchantress's rose fell. Was it too late?

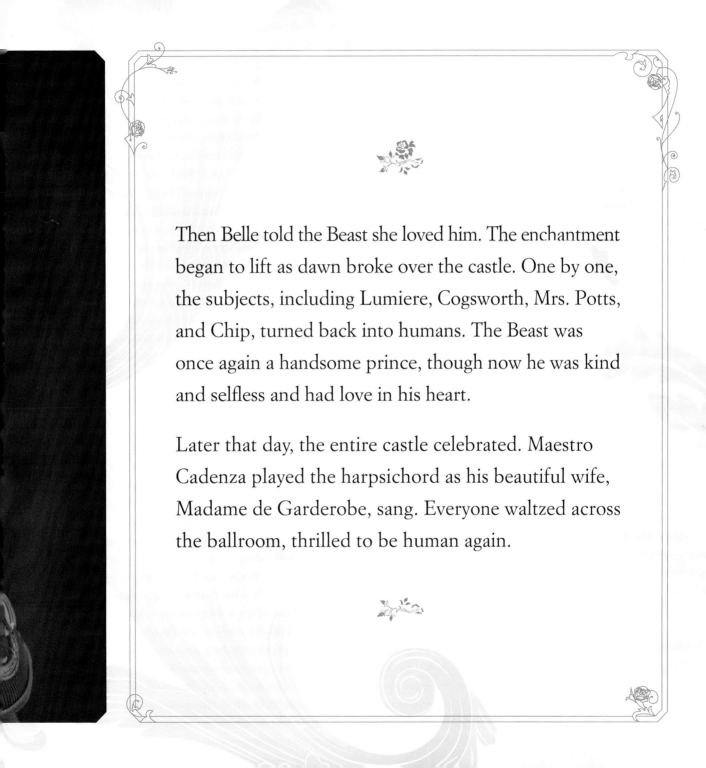

Then Belle told the Beast she loved him. The enchantment began to lift as dawn broke over the castle. One by one, the subjects, including Lumiere, Cogsworth, Mrs. Potts, and Chip, turned back into humans. The Beast was once again a handsome prince, though now he was kind and selfless and had love in his heart.

Later that day, the entire castle celebrated. Maestro Cadenza played the harpsichord as his beautiful wife, Madame de Garderobe, sang. Everyone waltzed across the ballroom, thrilled to be human again.

Belle was very happy that the Prince was alive and well. The enchantment over the castle might have lifted, but the enchantment of love between Belle and the Prince was just beginning.

It wasn't long before Belle turned the castle library into a schoolroom to teach boys and girls how to read. The Prince watched her with pride. They would have a wonderful, beautiful life together, fuller than Belle could ever have dreamed. She and the Prince had recognized the inner beauty in each other and would live happily ever after because of it.